Print a Book

written and illustrated by
Heinz Kurth

Puffin Books

Puffin Books: Penguin Books Ltd,
Harmondsworth, Middlesex, England
Penguin Books Inc.,
7110 Ambassador Road, Baltimore, Maryland 21207, U.S.A.
Penguin Books Australia Ltd,
Ringwood, Victoria, Australia
Penguin Books Canada Ltd,
41 Steelcase Road West, Markham, Ontario, Canada
Penguin Books (N.Z.) Ltd,
182–190 Wairau Road, Auckland 10, New Zealand

First published by Puffin Books 1975

Printed in Great Britain by
Colour Reproductions Ltd, Billericay, Essex, England

There are many different books which you can read.

But lots of people want to read the same book,
so thousands of copies of each are printed.

To begin with there is only one copy.
The words are written by an **author**,
the pictures are drawn by an **artist**,
and a **publisher** looks after the planning
and selling of the book.

Together they make a plan which shows
where the words and pictures will appear on each page.
The plan, the manuscript, and the pictures
are sent to a printing house.

The compositor types each word on a keyboard,
and the machine casts the words into lines of metal **type**.

Metal types have to be very strong so that they will not wear out when they are pressed on to paper thousands of times.

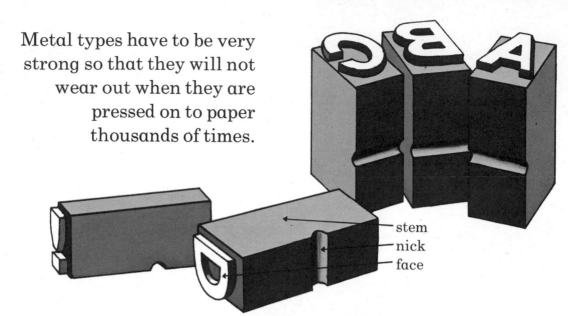

stem
nick
face

Do you see something odd? Types are always back to front so that when they are printed on paper the letters will appear the right way round.

There are different sizes of type
for printing letters
of different sizes.

NNNNN**N**N**N**

And there are types for printing figures . . .

0123456789

. . . as well as many other signs and symbols.

.,:-!?&

Do you know what they mean?

Words without spaces are difficult to read,
so metal blocks are put between the words to split them up.
They are lower than the letters and will not print.

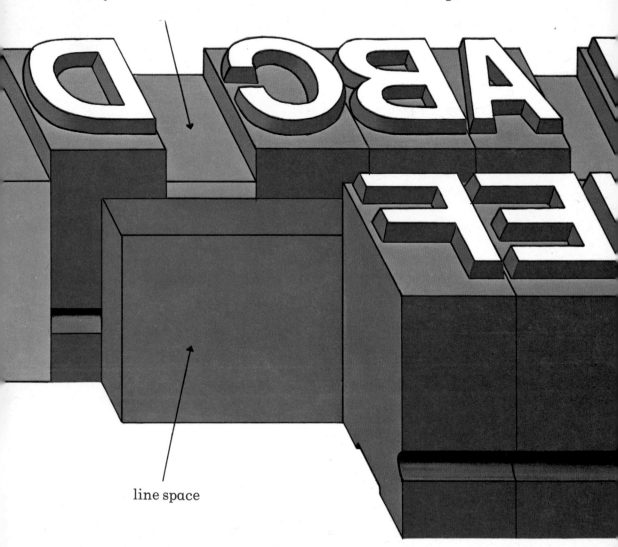

line space

While the words are being set,
the pictures are copied on to metal **plates**.

This picture
of a kitten
is made up of
black lines.

Like the metal types,
the picture on the plate
is back to front.
You can see that the lines
stand out from the plate.

The plate is called a **line block**
and is mounted on wood or metal.

The artist has drawn the picture on this page
in a different way to show the soft fur of the kitten.
How can grey shades be printed with solid black ink?

The picture is made into a pattern in which
the dark parts become big dots and the
light parts become small dots. Hold the
book away from you, and you will see how
the black dots and the white paper merge
into shades of grey. A plate which prints
shades of grey is called a **tone block**.

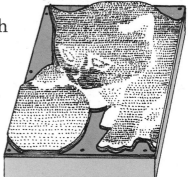

13

Tone blocks are also used to make colour pictures.
Four tone blocks are made, one each to print yellow,
red, blue and black. In the picture on the right
they were printed one on top of the other.

Yellow is printed first . . .   then the red . . .   and blue.

Overprinting makes more than four
colours – for instance when blue
is printed over yellow it makes green.
What colours would you need to make orange?

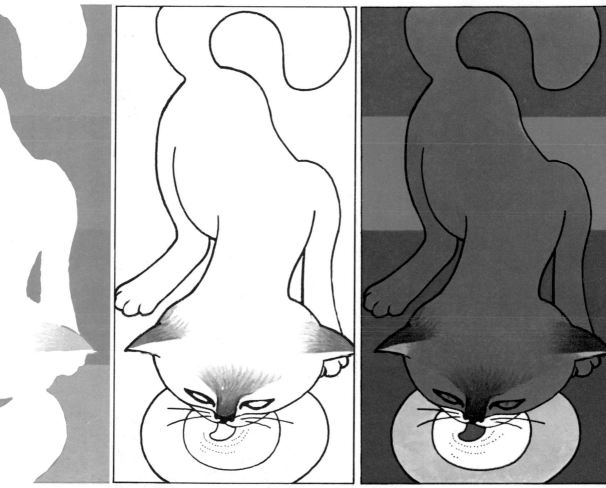

Black is the last colour.   All four colours are together.

frame   lock

The metal types and the picture blocks for the book
are ready. They are fitted into a steel **frame**.
The frame is placed on the **bed** of a printing machine.
Many pages will be printed at the same time
on a large sheet of paper.

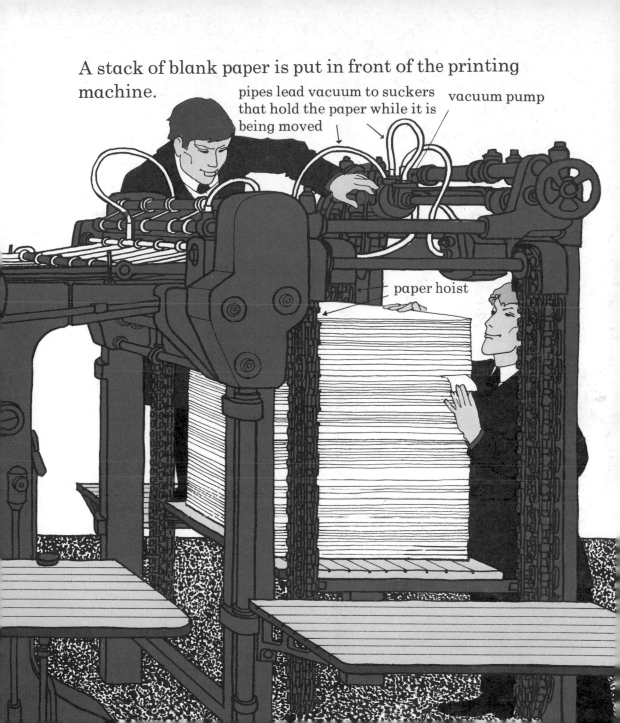

A stack of blank paper is put in front of the printing machine.

pipes lead vacuum to suckers that hold the paper while it is being moved

vacuum pump

paper hoist

The printer switches on the electric motor and the first sheet of paper is lifted on to the turning **cylinder**.
The bed carrying the frame with the type and blocks thunders backwards and forwards. At the same time the metal cylinder presses the paper on to the types and the pictures.
Each time the cylinder goes round a print is made.
The printed sheet is taken out and stacked.

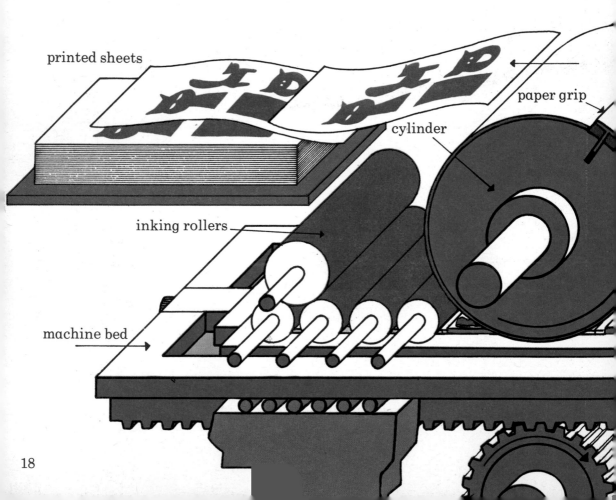

printed sheets

paper grip

cylinder

inking rollers

machine bed

A blank sheet of paper is pulled on to the cylinder. As the bed slides under the cylinder, the blocks are being inked.

The printed sheet is released and taken out. Then the cylinder is raised so that the bed can return and begin the next print.

blank paper

guide rails

motor

Printer's ink is thick and messy. It is taken from the **well** and passed from one roller to another so that by the time it is put on to the types and picture-blocks it is thin and silky.

well

type

PRINTING INK RED

Printing from letters
that stand out
is called **letterpress**.

But many books are printed
by machines which print
from a smooth plate
and are called **offset** presses.

The plate is curved around a cylinder and the ink
only sticks to the parts that are going to print.

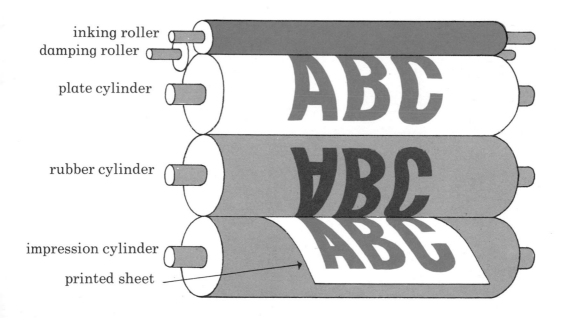

inking roller
damping roller

plate cylinder

rubber cylinder

impression cylinder

printed sheet

FOUR-COLOUR PRINTING MACHINE

printed
sheets
stacked

master printer
checks inking
and the register
of the colours

paper stacks
rest on pallets
so that they can
be moved by
a fork lift

This offset machine is as big as a house.

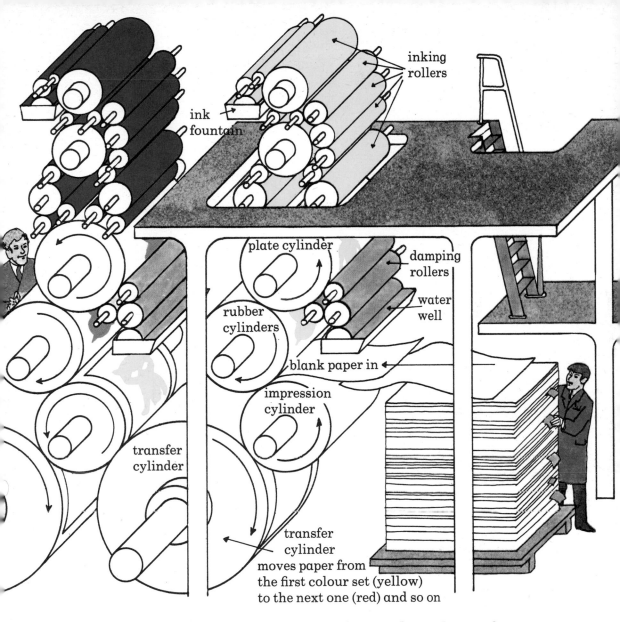

inking
rollers

ink
fountain

plate cylinder

damping
rollers

water
well

rubber
cylinders

blank paper in

impression
cylinder

transfer
cylinder

transfer
cylinder
moves paper from
the first colour set (yellow)
to the next one (red) and so on

It prints 4 colours one after the other and works so fast
that you can hardly see the paper shooting through.

front

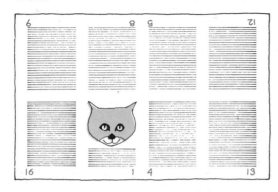

back

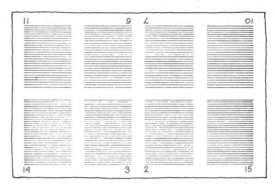

Now all the sheets for the book have been printed. Some of the pages are upside down and not in the right order.

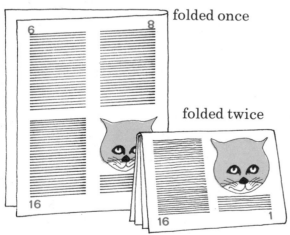

folded once

folded twice

and folded for the third time

But when the sheet is folded by the **binder** the pages will be in the right order and the right way up.

The folded sheets
are stitched with
thread to hold
the pages together.

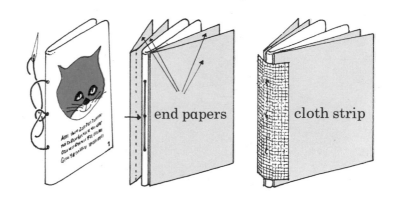

end papers

cloth strip

Two blank sheets of paper – the **end papers** –
are pasted to the edges of the first and last page,
and a strip of cloth is glued to the **spine**.
Then the pages are trimmed. The knife is so sharp
that it cuts the pages for several books at once.

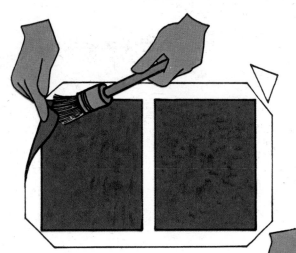

The book is going to have
a hard cover so that it will
last a long time. The cover
is made of stiff board.
The printed cover-paper
is pasted on to it
and folded over the edges.

The trimmed pages
are glued to the spine
of the cover
by the strip of cloth.

The two end papers
are pasted down
on to the front
and back covers
and the book
is finished.

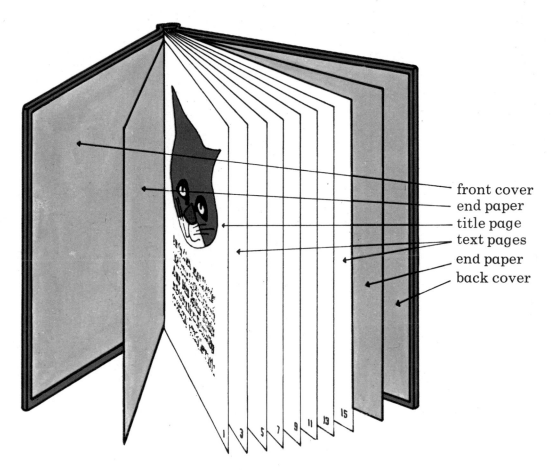

front cover
end paper
title page
text pages
end paper
back cover

The books are delivered to the publisher who sends them to bookshops and libraries all over the country.

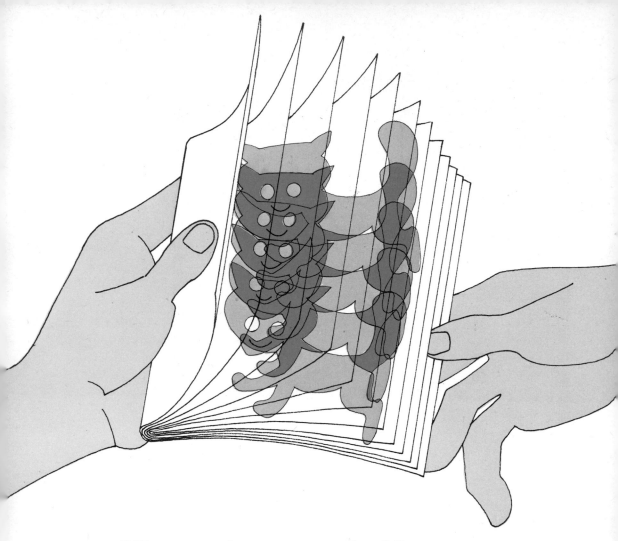

Why not print your own book?
Here is one in which a kitten jumps
when you flip the pages quickly. All you need
is *a potato, a knife, 3 sheets of paper, a needle and
thread, a brush* and some *water-colour paint.*

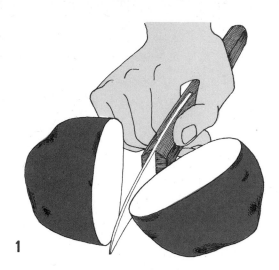

1

First cut the potato in half.

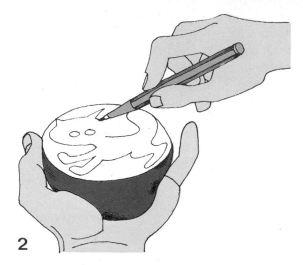

2

Then draw a kitten on it.

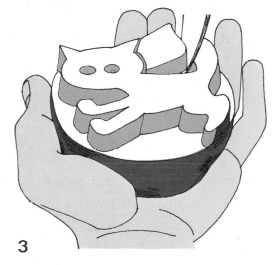

3

With the knife carefully cut away the potato around the kitten.

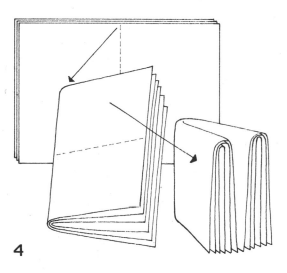

4

Now take the three sheets of paper, fold them in half and then in half again.

Some of the edges are still joined. Cut along the folds at the top.

5

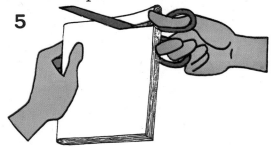

In pencil write *cover* on the outside sheet and number each page facing you.

6

Paint the cut-out shape on your potato.
Do not make it too wet.

7

8

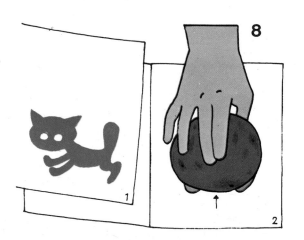

Press the potato firmly down in the middle of page 1.
Put it aside to dry.
Paint the potato again.
Press it down on page 2 but a little higher up the page than before.

9

Look how the kitten is printed a little higher on each page.
Do this on pages 3, 4, 5 and 6. Now print the
last five pages moving the kitten down again.

10

11

The Cover: Print the kitten
in one colour. Wash the potato,
and add another kitten
in a different colour.
Do this again.

Put all the pages together
in the right order and with
the needle and thread sew
along the spine as shown.
Tie the thread with a knot.

Your book is now ready. See how the kitten jumps as you flip the pages quickly!